CONTENTS

BOTTLED CITY
OF KANDOR

SUPERMAN™

TALES OF THE FORTRESS OF SOLITUDE

THE LAST CITY OF KRYPTON

by
MICHAEL DAHL

illustrated by
LUCIANO VECCHIO
& TIM LEVINS

Superman created by
JERRY SIEGEL AND JOE SHUSTER
BY SPECIAL ARRANGEMENT WITH
THE JERRY SIEGEL FAMILY

50000000040781

Raintree is an imprint of Capstone Global Library Limited, a company
incorporated in England and Wales having its registered office at 264
Banbury Road, Oxford, OX2 7DY – Registered company number: 6695582

www.raintree.co.uk
myorders@raintree.co.uk

STAR38655

Designed by Hilary Wacholz
Printed and bound in China

ISBN 978 1 4747 3948 1
21 20 19 18 17
10 9 8 7 6 5 4 3 2 1

British Library Cataloguing in Publication Data
A full catalogue record for this book is available from the British Library.

Behold the secret headquarters of Superman.

The Fortress of Solitude contains a lab, a museum, a zoo of alien creatures and thousands of trophies from the Man of Steel's adventures.

In one corner, Superman safely keeps the bottled city of Kandor in a protective case. Here's the tale behind that artifact . . .

CHAPTER 1

THE STOLEN CITY

A strange ship soars above the faraway planet Krypton.

The ship flies over the city of Kandor.

ZOOOOM!

As the ship moves closer, the citizens stare and point.

The ship seems to grow larger and larger.

Soon, the ship blocks the rays of the red sun from shining on the city.

"The ship is too big!" shouts a man in the street. "It will crush us!"

"No," says a woman standing nearby.

"The ship is not growing larger," she says. "Our city is getting smaller!"

The red sun disappears.

The people of Kandor scream and run in fright.

In place of the red sun, a giant green face appears in the sky.

An evil grin stretches high above
the buildings.

"Welcome," thunders the giant's voice.
"The city of Kandor has been captured by
my shrinking ray."

"You are now inside a glass bottle, where
you will stay forever."

The buildings of the city tremble at the
giant's laugh.

"You all belong to me . . . Brainiac!"

CHAPTER 2

A NEW TARGET

Many years later, and millions of miles away, the same ship nears Earth.

At the controls of his ship, Brainiac views the cities far below.

One city catches his attention – Metropolis.

Brainiac is a supercomputer in human form. He was built years ago on Krypton itself.

He has no feelings. He has no fear.

He is only filled with a desire for knowledge.

He collects cities throughout the universe to get it.

Brainiac prepares the controls.

"That city is the next prize for my collection," he says.

Brainiac's ship hovers above the city of Metropolis.

A red and blue blur flashes next to it in the sky.

It is Superman on patrol.

He has been keeping an eye on the strange ship.

Suddenly, a beam of light shoots from the bottom of the ship.

The city of Metropolis is covered in a green glow.

CHAPTER 3

SHRINKING RAY

Superman stares as Metropolis grows hazy in the strange green ray.

"The city is shrinking!" he says.

The Man of Steel flies towards the ship.

BAM!

An invisible barrier stops Superman from entering the ship.

There's only one way in, he thinks.

Superman flies into the ray.

He shrinks down along with the city
of Metropolis.

A giant green face appears above the city.

"You are all safe inside a glass bottle," says
Brainiac. "Where you will stay forever!"

Superman flies to the top of the huge bottle.

He uses his heat vision to melt the metal cap sealing them in.

The tiny Superman flies towards Brainiac and buzzes around the alien's head.

Brainiac swats at the bug-sized pest.

"What is that?" he cries.

With all his strength, Superman punches the alien's forehead.

Brainiac topples backwards onto the floor.

Sparks fly from his eyes and ears.

"He's a robot!" says Superman.

Superman rushes to the control panel.

He beams out his heat vision to fry the red button.

On the control screen, the hero watches as Metropolis grows larger again back on Earth.

"Uh-oh, that reminds me," says Superman.

He flies out of the ship and heads into the purple beam.

As Metropolis returns to its normal size, so does the Man of Steel.

"That was close," he says.

CHAPTER 4

OUT OF THE PAST

Superman is back to his normal size.

He soars up into the purple beam and enters the ship again.

The control room is empty.

Where has the robot enemy gone?

"I'm over here, Kal-El," comes an evil voice.

Superman spins around and sees Brainiac standing behind him in another room.

"Why did you call me that?" asks Superman. "That was the name my parents gave me on Krypton."

"I knew your father, Jor-El," says Brainiac. "As soon as I saw you, I knew you were the son of Krypton's greatest scientist."

"I am from Krypton too," he says.

"It doesn't matter where you're from," says Superman. "You're going to prison."

Superman closes in on his enemy.

He draws back his fist for another awesome punch.

He knows he can knock out Brainiac's circuits.

Brainiac suddenly pulls out a weapon.

He aims it at a nearby bottle.

"Stop!" he shouts. "Or I will destroy the last piece of our home planet."

CHAPTER 5

THE LAST OF KRYPTON

Superman sees a shrunken city inside the bottle.

"A city from Krypton!" he says.

"It's called Kandor," says Brainiac. "If you don't leave my ship, I'll destroy the entire bottle."

"But there are hundreds of people living in there," says Superman.

"Thousands," says Brainiac coldly.

"Maybe destroying the city is too much," he adds. "Maybe, instead, I'll do this!"

Brainiac slams a switch on a nearby wall.

A hatch opens on the side of his ship, and the bottled city is tossed into the air by a mechanical spring.

"Farewell, Kal-El," says Brainiac with a grin.

Superman frowns. It only takes him a second to fly out of the hatch after the falling city.

The Man of Steel dives through the sky.

Behind him, Brainiac's ship powers its jets. It streams into space, leaving Earth far behind.

Meanwhile, Superman reaches the falling city of Kandor.

His hands carefully grab onto the bottle.

Then he gently touches down on the streets of Metropolis. The bottle is cradled in his arms.

"Welcome to your new home," says Superman.

EPILOGUE . . .

"Someday I'll find a way to return you to normal size," says Superman.

Superman gazes into the bottle, and the people inside see a new gigantic face.

To the people of Kandor, it's not the face of Superman. It looks like the face of Jor-El, the scientist.

"If anyone can help us, he can!" they say. "Like father, like son."

GLOSSARY

circuit path for electricity to flow through

citizen member of a particular city

desire strong wish or need for something

hatch covered hole in a floor, deck, wall or ceiling

knowledge information that someone or something knows

Krypton Superman's home planet

mechanical operated by machinery

supercomputer large, very fast computer usually used for scientific research

universe Earth, the planets, the stars and all things in space

DISCUSS

1. Could Superman have saved Kandor without being shrunk down himself? Explain your answer.

2. Brainiac collects cities throughout the universe. Do you collect anything? Discuss your collections.

3. Do you believe Superman will fulfil his promise to return Kandor to its normal size? Why or why not?

WRITE

1. Super heroes are often big, strong and muscular. List some advantages to being a microscopic hero.

2. Imagine being shrunk down to the size of an ant. Write a story about your miniature adventures!

3. Write your own tale of Superman. What villain will the hero face next? Who will he save? The choice is up to you!

AUTHOR

Michael Dahl is the author of more than 200 titles for young adults and children, including *The Last Son of Krypton*. He once saw and touched the very first Superman comic book. He is now convinced that he came from another planet and was adopted by his current parents, but they're not giving anything away.

ILLUSTRATORS

Luciano Vecchio was born in 1982 and is based in Buenos Aires, Argentina. He has illustrated many DC Super Heroes books for Capstone, and his recent comic work includes *Beware the Batman*, *Green Lantern: The Animated Series*, *Young Justice*, *Ultimate Spider-Man* and his creator-owned webcomic, *Sereno*.

Tim Levins is best known for his work on the Eisner Award-winning DC Comics series *Batman: Gotham Adventures*. Tim has illustrated other DC titles, such as *Justice League Adventures*, *Batgirl*, *Metal Men* and *Scooby-Doo*, and has also done work for Marvel Comics and Archie Comics. Tim enjoys life in Midland, Ontario, Canada, with his wife, son, dog and two horses.